Mary Lee Donovan

Lian Cho

A Hundred Thousand Welcomes

WITHDRAWN

Greenwillow Books

An Imprint of HarperCollins*Publishers*

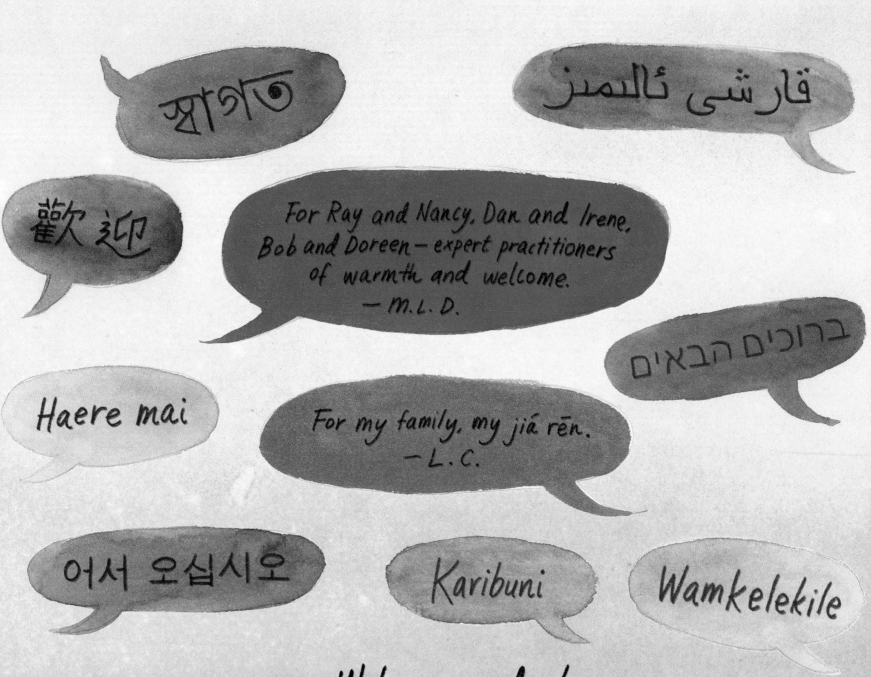

স্বাগত

قارشى ئالمىز

歡迎

For Ray and Nancy, Dan and Irene,
Bob and Doreen — expert practitioners
of warmth and welcome.
— M. L. D.

ברוכים הבאים

Haere mai

For my family, my jiá rēn.
— L. C.

어서 오십시오

Karibuni

Wamkelekile

Welcome, reader!

The text of this book is written as a poem. Written into the poem are several translations of the English word *welcome*. Each should be read, in order, as part of the poem. Pronunciation guides are tucked into the artwork and are loosely based on the International Phonetic Alphabet (IPA). Bold-faced type indicates which syllables should be stressed. This key to approximate vowel sounds should also help. You will find additional information about the featured languages at the end of the book.

/a/ is the vowel in *chai* /i/ is the vowel in *eat*
/æ/ is the vowel in *bat* /ɪ/ is the vowel in *hip*
/ɑ/ is the vowel in *ball* /o/ is the vowel in *coal*
/ɛ/ is the vowel in *bet* or *boy*
/e/ is the vowel in *pear* /u/ is the vowel in *boot*
/ə/ is the vowel in *the* /ʊ/ is the vowel in *put*

ようこそ

"I will welcome the stranger."

There are almost as many ways of making someone feel welcome as there are people on the planet. To welcome another is to give that person and yourself a chance at a new connection, a new friendship, and maybe even new eyes through which to view the world. Just as there are many customs for extending hospitality to others, there are thousands of ways to say *Welcome*, too.

The call to welcome the stranger and to offer peace and refuge—aman— to those in danger is deeply rooted in ancient traditions and in all major religions. The truth is that "we are all migrants on this earth, journeying together in hope." In one place or another, at one time or another, in one way or another, every single one of us will find ourselves in search of acceptance, help, protection, *welcome*.

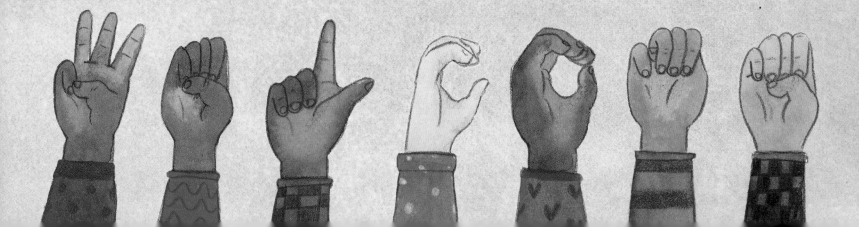

Welcome, friend.

Welcome.

Dear neighbor, come in.

No stranger dwells here;
I greet you as kin.

The door is wide open—
come in from the storm.

We'll shelter in peace,
break bread where it's warm.

Hellos and *How-are-yous*,
ancient and young.

I bow to your spirit.

Selamat datang.

salamat datang

Ahlan wa sahlan.

Bienvenida.

byembenida

hwæn ying

Huānyíng.

I greet you in sunshine
or by light of the moon.

My house is your house,
oh, most honored guest.

Yōkoso,

yokoso

shāgata.

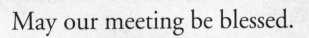

May our meeting be blessed.

Water to drink,
to wash dust from your feet.

Bread and salt,
honey . . . our fellowship feast.

Tell me your stories,
sing me your songs.

Life has more flavor
since you came along.

Willkommen,

vɪlkomən

svāgat,

khush āmdīd.

Aman

is here, where
the lanterns are lit.

aemæn.

or *säläm biryem.*

sælæm biryem

never know hunger.

May you

In any language,
welcome without end.

Céad míle fáilte.

This blessing I give:

ked melə falchə

fill your nights.

grow strong in the light.

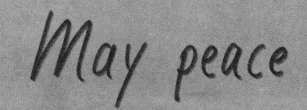

May peace

May your children's children

May the road rise to meet you,
and walls fall away.

A hundred thousand welcomes

I sing,
I sign,
I pray.

A Note from the Author

I am not a marcher. I am not a rally-er. I am not a fist shaker. I am not a knitter of hats or a waver of signs. My rage boils down, instead, to ink. This particular river of ink is my love song to our shared humanity and it is my protest against intolerance, injustice, and inhumanity.

When I was first moved to write this book, I started simply: find out how to say *Welcome* in as many languages as possible. That search showed me that language travels and changes as people travel and mingle—clear proof that we are connected across time and place.

After I completed the language research, I looked into customs of welcome around the world. Every custom, every symbol, every metaphor for welcome that I found exploded into even more amazing facts and connections. I knew then that the text I wrote would have to do the same: behind almost every single word I chose lies a world of information and meaning that can be explored if one wants to dig deeper.—M. L. D.

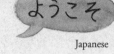
Japanese

Hebrew

Xhosa

A Note from the Artist

Food is something that joins us across cultures. We all eat it; we all cook it; we welcome friends, family, and strangers with it; and we all come together over meals. When this story first reached me, I knew that I wanted some aspect of this book to revolve around food. Families from all over the world joyfully coming together and welcoming strangers across a giant table filled with delicious foods from many cultures felt like the right thing to paint in a time when hate and fear are championed.

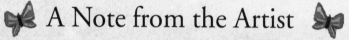
Swahili

We fear what we do not know, and I hope that through these pages, readers will learn more about cultures and families and rituals different from their own. From the beginning, I knew that I wanted to paint real people and real families, not the stereotypes that exist online or are imbedded in our imaginations. Our world is diverse, and our world is beautiful, but it was difficult to find references that supported that, beyond standard stock photos and other images that enforce stereotypes. I had to be creative and determined. I toured the streets of Bangladesh virtually, watched home videos of people being welcomed for tea in Bashkortostan, and spoke with many friends who grew up in many places, in an attempt to get a glimpse into the real homes of real families.

Korean

I hope I did these families justice, and I hope you will find something new and inspiring within these pages, as I did. I hope you will feel welcome.

This book is dedicated to my family: to my mother, who took care of my sister and me when we moved from Taiwan to New Zealand; to my father, who stayed in Taiwan to work and provide for us; and to my grandma, who passed away while I was working on these paintings. This book is dedicated to my jiá rēn, who can be found on page fourteen.—L. C.

Maori

Chinese

Bengali

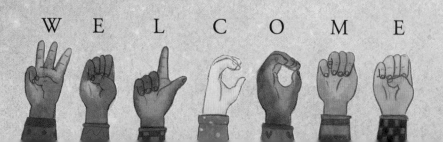
Uyghur

W E L C O M E

A Note about Pronunciation

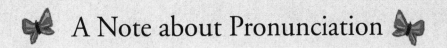

Languages, like people, travel. Some of the most commonly spoken languages in the world appear in this book. This is a tiny fraction of the approximately 7000 languages and dialects spoken today. Of the 7000 total languages, 40 percent are in danger of disappearing altogether when their remaining speakers are gone or when the language is no longer customarily used by children. The total number of speakers noted here for each language is a combination of those who are native speakers and those who use it as their second language.

Below each word (or words) of welcome is a phonetic spelling to help you pronounce them correctly. To write a pronunciation phonetically means to write it using a system of letters and symbols that tell us how a vowel or consonant or combination of letters is meant to sound when we speak it aloud. Bold-faced type indicates which syllables should be stressed. Linguists and phoneticians—scientists who study language—developed the International Phonetic Alphabet (IPA) to make it possible for people all over the world to understand how words in different languages sound when spoken. This book uses a system inspired by the IPA, but simplified to make it more accessible to readers.

In order of
appearance:

welcome
English
[**wɛl**kəm]
Number of speakers:
more than 1.2 trillion

selamat datang
Indonesian
[sələmət da**tang**]
Number of speakers:
more than 198 million

ahlan wa sahlan
Modern Standard Arabic
[æhlæn wæ **sæh**læn]
Number of speakers:
more than 273 million

bienvenida
Spanish/Castilian
[byembe**ni**da]
Number of speakers:
more than 537 million

huānyíng
Mandarin (Chinese)
[hwæn ying]
Number of speakers:
more than 1.1 trillion

yōkoso
Japanese
[**yo**koso]
Number of speakers:
more than 125 million

shāgata
Bengali
[**sha**goto]
Number of speakers:
more than 265 million

willkommen
German, Standard
[vɪl**kom**ən]]
Number of speakers:
more than 131 million

svāgat
Hindi
[**sva**gət]
Number of speakers:
more than 637 million

khush āmdid
aman (means "peace and refuge")
Modern Standard Urdu
[**hʊsh** ɑm**did**]
[**æmæn**]
Number of speakers:
more than 170 million

tanyán yahípi
Lakota Sioux
[tənyən ya**hi**pi]
Endangered
Number of speakers:
approximately 2200

säläm biryem
Bashkir/Bashkort
[sælæm bi**ryem**]
Number of speakers:
more than 1.2 million

Céad míle fáilte
Gaelic/Irish
[**ked** melə **fɑl**chə]
Endangered
Number of speakers:
more than 1.2 million

On p. 3: "I will welcome the stranger" and "we are all migrants on this earth, journeying together in hope" are quotes from *Welcoming the Stranger: Affirmations for Faith Leaders.* (See below.)

Selected Sources

ACLED (Armed Conflict Location & Event Data Project [associated with the International Peace Research Institute (PRIO)] https://acleddata.com/about-acled/

Ager, Simon. "Omniglot-writing systems and languages of the world." 3rd January 2021. www.omniglot.com

CRED (Centre for Research on the Epidemiology of Disasters). "Human cost of disasters. An overview of the last 20 years 2000–2019." https://reliefweb.int/report/world/human-cost-disasters-overview-last-20-years-2000-2019

Eberhard, David M., Gary F. Simons, and Charles D. Fennig (eds.). 2020. *Ethnologue: Languages of the World.* Twenty-third edition. Dallas, TX: SIL International. Online version: http://www.ethnologue.com

Institute of Global Homelessness. https://ighomelessness.org

International Phonetic Association. www.internationalphoneticassociation.org

International Rescue Committee. https://www.rescue.org/

Ladefoged, Peter and Ian Maddieson. *The Sounds of the World's Languages.* (Cambridge, Mass.: Blackwell Publishers, Inc., 1996).

UN-Habitat. https://unhabitat.org/topic/housing

US Committee for Refugees and Immigrants (USCRI). https://refugees.org/

Welcoming the Stranger: Affirmations for Faith Leaders. UNHCR, The UN Refugee Agency. http://www.unhcr.org/51b6de419.html

A Selection of Further Reading for Young Readers

Agee, Jon. *The Wall in the Middle of the Book.* Illustrated by the author. New York: Penguin Random House/Dial Books for Young Readers, 2018. (Ages 4–8)

Alva, Alfredo with Deborah Mills. *La Frontera: El viaje con papá/My Journey with Papa.* Illustrated by Claudia Navarro. Cambridge, MA: Barefoot Books, 2018. (Ages 4–8)

Bates, Juniper. *The Big Umbrella.* Illustrated by Amy June Bates. New York: Simon & Schuster/Paula Wiseman Books, 2018. (Ages 4–8)

Danticat, Edwidge. *Mama's Nightingale: A Story of Immigration and Separation.* Illustrated by Leslie Staub. New York: Penguin Young Readers Group, 2015. (Ages 5–8)

de Arias, Patricia. *Marwan's Journey.* Illustrated by Laura Borràs. Hong Kong: minedition/ Michael Neugebauer Publishing Ltd., 2018. (Ages 5–7)

Jeffers, Oliver. *What We'll Build: Plans for Our Together Future.* Illustrated by the author. New York: Penguin Young Readers Group, 2020. (Ages 4–8)

Kerascoët. *I Walk with Vanessa: A Story about a Simple Act of Kindness.* Illustrated by the author. New York: Schwartz & Wade/Penguin Random House, 2018. (Ages 4–8)

Kuntz, Doug and Amy Shrodes. *Lost and Found Cat: The True Story of Kunkush's Incredible Journey.* Illustrated by Sue Cornelison. New York: Penguin Random House/Crown Books for Young Readers, 2017. (Ages 4–8)

Meddour, Wendy. *Lubna and Pebble.* Illustrated by Daniel Egnéus. New York: Penguin Young Readers Group, 2019. (Ages 4–8)

Méndez, Yamile Saied. *Where Are You From?* Illustrated by Jaime Kim. New York: HarperCollins Publishers, 2019. (Ages 4–8)

Morales, Yuyi. *Dreamers.* Illustrated by the author. New York: Neal Porter Books/Roaring Brook Press, 2018. (Ages 4–8)

Penfold, Alexandra. *All Are Welcome.* Illustrated by Suzanne Kaufman. New York: Knopf Books for Young Readers, 2018. (Ages 4–8)

Ruurs, Margriet. *Stepping Stones: A Refugee Family's Journey.* Illustrated by Nizar Ali Badr. Translated from the Arabic by Falah Raheem. English and Arabic edition. Custer, WA: Orca Book Publishers, 2016. (Ages 6–8)

Sanna, Francesca. *The Journey.* London: Flying Eye Books/Nobrow, 2016. (Ages 5–7)

Woodson, Jacqueline. *The Day You Begin.* Illustrated by Rafael López. New York: Simon & Schuster/Nancy Paulsen Books, 2018. (Ages 5–8)

Thank you to Alexander Elias, PhD student in the Department of Linguistics, University of California, Berkeley.

Library of Congress Cataloging-in-Publication Data is available. ISBN 978-0-06-287772-7 (hardback)

21 22 23 24 25 RTLO 10 9 8 7 6 5 4 3 2 1 First Edition   Greenwillow Books